MW01134322

Amy's Ulu

Iñupiat Heritage Series

Written By
Linda L. Beck

Cover illustration by
Maryna Voloshyna

Inside illustration by
Selah Pansariang

Illustration by Selah Pansariang

Special thanks to the people of Kotzebue and to the nearby villages
for sharing their way of life with me as a child. They made my life
rich with experiences that are eternally precious.

Glossary is included in the front of the book for understanding.

Scripture is in The New Living Translation.

Amy's Ulu

Iñupiat Heritage Series

By

Linda L. Beck

Dedicated to
the children of Kotzebue
and villages beyond,
to see their future with wisdom.

Special thanks to
Summer Frisk and Heidi Hauser,
my daughters,
for their help in bringing this book to completion.

Special acknowledgements to
Maryna Voloshyna
for the original painting of
Amy and Aukluk on the cover.

Special thanks to
Selah Pansariang,
my Granddaughter, for the original
sketch of Amy inside the book.

Special thanks to
Anthony Henry of Anchorage
who made the authentic Iñupiat ulus
for the book.

Glossary

Mukluks:	Winter boots made out of fur and leather and worn for winter weather.
Muktuk:	An Iñupiat food from a Beluga whale or Black whale.
Ulu:	Half circle shaped knife.
Ruff:	A fur rim around a hood on a parka.
Sinew:	A type of thread made from caribou or reindeer.
Bone needle:	Sewing needle made out of bone.
Leather thimble:	A thimble used to protect fingers while sewing with a bone needle.
Seal oil:	A type of oil used for cooking and eating.
Pilot Bread Crackers:	A type of round cracker commonly eaten in the place of bread in the Arctic.

Salmon Berries:	An orange colored berry, similar to a blackberry that grows wild in Alaska.
Marrow:	A fatty edible food inside of a bone.
Eskimo Ice-cream:	A type of ice-cream made with fat, berries and sugar, whipped into a substance that is frozen and used as ice-cream. It comes with different kinds of berries or even fish.
"Addii"	A phrase that means essentially, "Oh my!" It is an expression often used as an exclamation when surprised or pleased.
Baleen:	The hard substance inside of a whale's mouth that strains plankton for the whale to eat.
White-out:	A condition where snow and sky meet in a completely white state, usually during a blowing snow storm. It is a dangerous weather situation where visibility is almost non-existent.
Set nets:	Long fishing nets set out in a line to catch fish in a river or the ocean.

Contents

C H A P T E R   O N E

The Fourth of July!

Amy smiled as she slipped her summer parka over her T-shirt and jeans. Today was the Fourth of July. It was her favorite day of the whole year, except for Christmas.

Amy picked up her long scarf and wrapped it quickly around her waist. Her little brother, Isaac, toddled over and Amy picked him up. It was her job to watch him today, so she flipped him up on to her back so that she could carry him. She leaned forward and tied the scarf carefully under his bottom and around to the front of her parka, securing a knot. He sat forward against her back and waved his fat brown arms and giggled with delight.

Amy's mom, Esther, worked as a nurse at the hospital. She was on her shift that holiday. Amy's dad, George, was out fishing and staying with their family in the village of Kiana, so Amy was on her own. She also had another brother, Sam, who was two years younger than she was. He was outside playing with his friends.

Amy's cousin, Bea, was working at the celebration, so Amy walked toward the donut stand where Bea was frying donuts. She watched her dip the big hunk of hot fried bread into sugar, which she handed to Amy.

Isaac leaned forward and pulled Amy's hair to get her attention. She handed him a piece of the donut and he shoved it quickly into his mouth. As soon as he ate it, he started crying for more. Amy split it in half and he happily ate it, while smearing sugar on her braid with his fat, dimpled hands. She brushed the sugar off her braids and smiled with happiness. She loved the Fourth of July!

The fun holiday began with the village kids competing in the foot races. They were lining up now. Amy walked over to watch the boys from her school lean over the starting line, ready to run. After this race would come the three legged race, the muktuk * eating contest and the skin toss. The day was fun and full of food and prizes and would end late into the night.

The celebrations would go on late because the sun didn't really disappear in the summertime. It dipped only slightly on the horizon and it stayed light all night because Kotzebue was so far north, above the Arctic Circle. Everyone would stay up until early morning.

Kotzebue was a small town, but larger than the villages up the river. Amy knew almost everyone in town. Various people might come and go, but the ones who lived there all the time knew each other well. Most were family or felt like family.

To the left, the women from town were stepping forward for the Baby Beauty contest. They would show off their fur parkas, trimmed with geometric reindeer and caribou skin designs. The parkas had wolf and wolverine ruffs* around the hoods and strips of squirrel or muskrat fur which hung down the front and back of the fur skin parka.

The women all carried babies on their backs, who were dressed in rabbit fur parkas with mukluks* on their feet. It was a chance for everyone to see all the new little babies of the village up to the age of two, who were dressed up for the contest in beautiful new fur parkas.

Amy smiled and waved at her Aunt Jessica, who had her year-old baby girl on her back. Aunt Jessica and her mom had sewn the parkas that they were wearing for this contest. She hoped her aunt's baby, Minnie, would win, as she was definitely the cutest baby of all, dressed in her white rabbit fur parka and soft brown mukluks.

Amy waved at her and Minnie's chubby brown face smiled with dimples in her cheeks. She was a happy baby.

Isaac laughed and pointed and tried to stand up on Amy's back in his excitement to see Minnie. He dug his heels in, trying to see. Amy shifted him a bit to get more comfortable.

Jennifer, a friend of Amy's from school, saw her and came running over.

"Amy!" You 'gotta come over and see what I have!" Jennifer gasped with excitement. "I got it today!"

"What is it?" Amy asked.

"Come and see!" Jennifer voice pitched with excitement.

Jennifer pulled on the sleeve of Amy's parka, guiding her away from the Fourth of July celebration toward her cabin.

"Wait!" Amy said. "I need to see if Sam can watch Isaac for a few minutes.

The two girls searched for Sam and found him watching Iñupiat dancing. Amy slid Isaac off her back and handed him over.

"I'll be back in a few minutes," she told Sam as she kissed Isaac's donut-sugary cheek good-bye.

Amy followed Jennifer away from the celebrations, down to Front Street where she lived. Jennifer rounded the corner and pulled Amy toward the house. Amy's curiosity was growing. *What was it?* She wondered. When she got close to the house, her eyes opened wide with excitement. She couldn't believe her eyes!

Amy's Ulu

R ight beside Jennifer's house, was a snowmobile, a dog-sled, buckets of seal oil, * and strips of meat and fish hanging on drying racks. There was an old Jeep, from fifteen years back that was fading from red to light pink, with the hood and the two back tires missing. What made Amy gasp with excitement, was the shiny red motor scooter that was parked by the front door.

"Is that yours?" Amy gasped.

"Yah! My dad ordered it from Anchorage and we just got it! My Dad said it is mine, but it is for my family too," Jennifer said with joy.

Amy went over and put her hands on the handlebars.

"Can you take me for a ride?" Amy asked with excitement.

"Let me go and ask Papa," Jennifer replied.

She ran through the storm porch and into the house.

A few minutes later, Jennifer reappeared and said, "Papa said we could drive up to the lagoon, but that we have to come back soon."

The two girls climbed on the scooter and Jennifer started the engine. The engine started with a powerful sound and they laughed with delight as they spun out on the gravel, heading down Front Street, past the store and church, toward the lagoon. Neighbors smiled and waved as they whizzed by.

A couple of their school friends hollered out when they saw them, "Hey, take us for a ride!"

Amy waved as they went by. The wind whistled in their ears as they flew down the road. Everyone was still at the Fourth of July celebration so the lagoon was quiet. They got off the scooter and looked back at the town. A stray dog wandered by and waves were rippling over the water. They threw a couple of rocks across the lagoon to see if they could skip them. After about ten minutes they decided to head back.

Amy jumped on the seat behind Jennifer and as she did, she noticed to the right that there was a bag caught on a branch of willows. She tapped Jennifer on the shoulder, jumped off the scooter and ran over to see what it was. A reindeer skin bag hung around a skinny branch. It had a flap and beading around the edge.

She reached for it and unwrapped it from the branch.

"Look, Jennifer!"

The two girls could see that the bag was beautifully made of reindeer skin with beaded designs sewn on the flap.

"Someone must have lost it! Shall we open it and see what is inside?" Amy asked with curiosity.

They looked at each other and then Amy quickly opened the front flap to look. Amy reached inside and pulled out four things: an Iñupiat sewing kit with sinew thread,* a bone needle,* a hard leather thimble* and an ulu,* which is a type of Iñupiat knife. This ulu made them gasp with surprise. This was not a common ulu. It had words on the ivory handle. They were surprised to see the writing on it.

The words said,

"For the Word of God is quick and powerful."
Heb. 4:12

Beneath that is said,

"He who holds this, holds power."

"Wow!" Amy exclaimed. "What do you think it means?"

She looked at Jennifer with surprise and wonder.

"I don't know..." whispered Jennifer with wonder, "It's not like my mother's ulu! We better go back now. Maybe we can ask your mom about it. Besides, we have to find out who lost it."

Amy put the handle of the bag over her shoulder and clutched it under her arm tightly for the ride back. She jumped on the motor scooter again. They drove back, with the wind whipping their hair.

Amy carried the bag carefully back to the Fourth of July celebration area, looking for Sam and Isaac. She located them and they bought some cotton candy together. Isaac was tired and needed a nap so Amy decided to walk home. She put him up on her back, tied up the scarf to hold him on under her parka cover and started for home. Isaac nodded asleep as Amy walked.

Suddenly she had a terrifying thought. It made her shudder.

What if the ulu had something to do with black magic?

She trembled, thinking about it.

It did say, He who holds this holds power!

She was suddenly afraid.

What if the ulu was cursed? What if it belonged to an evil person!

Her thoughts ran wild. Just when she was imagining a dark, scary figure casting a spell using the ulu, a loud, explosive bang made her jump!

She screamed with terror!

CHAPTER THREE

Fire!

T he bang had come from Front Street not far from Jennifer's house. Smoke billowed up from the area. Amy and Jennifer could hear people running from the celebration area and shouting about a fire.

They ran toward the fire. Amy could see flames shooting high into the air from a house close to the store. The fire crackled and popped loudly. Flames rose upward from the roof, curling around the eaves and into the bright sky. Black smoke billowed out of a hole in the roof.

She knew it was the house of one of the elders in the village. His name was Abe. He lived alone and was very old. She didn't see him there and looked around. People were bringing buckets of water and she could hear a fire truck coming with a wailing siren. Someone must have called for help.

Where was Abe? she thought.

He was nowhere to be seen and people were looking around toward the back of the house for him.

His dog came running from behind the house, with a chain dangling from her neck, whining. The dog had jerked herself free from the stake and chain which held her near her doghouse. She had somehow pulled it hard enough to get away from the fire. She ran down the road, tail between her legs, whimpering in fear.

The smoke grew blacker and it smelled like stove oil. The house was going up in flames and when the firetruck arrived, the house was already caving in from the fire. *There was no saving it now!* Amy thought. No one knew where Abe was. No one wanted to say, but they hoped was that he was not inside.

People stood around asking each other where he might be.

They were whispering, "Maybe he is out fishing or picking berries…"

No one seemed to have seen him in the last few hours.

The church bell was ringing. More and more people came to see what the bell was ringing for. It was used to alert people to come and help to put out fires.

A four-wheeler ATV roared up and stopped near the house. To everyone's relief, Abe was sitting behind the driver. People sighed and started talking to Abe and asking him where he had been.

"I was at church," he exclaimed. "I went to find my Bible, because I forgot it last Sunday."

He smiled. "I guess God saved my life!" He continued, "It is ok, at least I have my jacket and my pants."

He looked sadly at the house. "Maybe I will have to stay with somebody."

Amy's mom had just arrived from work with Isaac and Sam. She took a look at the fire and Abe and said, "Uncle," (which she called all male elders of the village out of respect,) "you can stay with us."

Amy looked up at her mom and smiled. She was glad that her mom was always helping people. Amy liked Abe too and felt bad for him. She was glad that he would be staying with them for awhile.

Then she remembered the ulu in the bag she was carrying. She was suddenly afraid. The ulu had power.

What if the fire happened because she took the ulu?

Her hands shook as she reached down for it.

Where was it? Her thoughts became suddenly fearful again.

She finally felt the shape of the ulu. It was there but she wasn't sure she should have taken it from the lagoon.

Summer Camp and Muskrats

A my got home and hid the skin purse and ulu inside her blanket on the bed. She wanted to tell her mom about it, but her mom was busy getting Abe settled into their house. She was making him some soup and gave him some dried fish and tea. Amy waited patiently and held Isaac who was munching on Saltine crackers.

Abe was talking about his house and Mom was listening. Amy waited to bring up the ulu, but it didn't seem right while they were talking about the fire. Abe continued to talk about his loss. He said he didn't lose that much, but he wanted to know where his dog Mika was.

Amy told him that his dog ran away from the fire and Abe was glad to hear that, saying she would come back looking for food. After that, Abe laid down to take a rest after his exhausting day.

Mom began to wash the dishes so Amy ran to the bed to get the skin bag. She brought it out and told her mom the whole story.

Mom paused and replied, "Don't worry. I will ask around and find out whom it belongs to."

Amy wanted to say something about how scared she was of the ulu, but it seemed silly now. She was thinking about it and it didn't register that Mom was talking about going camping the next day. Finally, she heard what Mom was saying.

"We are going to fish camp tomorrow by Kiana." Mom said.

She was talking about their fishing camp and how they were going to go across Kobuk Lake to fish upriver the next day. That sounded like fun. Abe would go too and they would take their big river boat with Uncle Joe to meet Amy's dad, George, near the village of Kiana at their camp.

Amy ran to pack her bag. She threw in a book, jacket, boots, clothes and at last, the bag with the ulu.

*Just in case…*she thought. She felt responsible for it, somehow.

The next morning was chilly and raining slightly. Amy pulled on an extra sweater to wear under her rain jacket. She sprayed on some mosquito repellent for the trip and put on her jacket and boots.

She knew it would be a wet and wild ride, since Kobuk Lake always acted like caribou running across the tundra, jumping around wild and free. It was always windy and very rough.

Amy's uncle, Joe, came by and loaded the fishing equipment, barrels of fuel, dried fish, rice and the tent. Blankets, diapers for Isaac, jackets, canned milk, bags of sugar, coffee and more food went on top. They threw a tarp over it all for protection from the rain.

They took the truck and pulled the boat down to the lagoon with Uncle Joe, Uncle Abe, Mom, Sam, Isaac, Amy and her puppy, Aukluk and also, Abe's dog, Mika, who had returned during the night. They all piled into the boat. Uncle Joe shoved the boat into the water, started the motor and the boat slowly headed out.

The boat motored out of the lagoon and toward Kobuk Lake. After about half an hour, the boat was slamming up and down and the icy waves were splashing in. The waves were high and soon they were all cold and soaked.

Amy pulled the tarp over her legs, tucking Isaac underneath and she hung on. It was always a *'grit your teeth and hang on'* type of ride across Kobuk Lake. The two dogs were whining at the rough ride, but Isaac was wrapped in a blanket under the tarp, so he was warm and dry. Sam hung on to the seat, grinning. He liked the wild and windy adventure. Mom had a raincoat on over her jacket and Uncle Abe had a jacket and baseball cap on to protect his face from the rain. Uncle Joe was at the back, driving.

He was used to many days of fishing on the lake and seemed comfortable with the weather.

The boat bounced its way through the whitecaps and swells and finally entered the river head. Immediately it was quieter. Everyone sighed and Amy threw the tarp off and let the warmth of the sun seep through her wet clothes.

Aukluk, her puppy, climbed on her lap and licked her face, shaking dirty water all over her. She yelled at him and told him to sit still. Mom reached for the thermos and poured some coffee for each of them to drink for warmth.

Abe said, "We'll be there soon!"

Sure enough, in about an hour, Uncle Joe slowed the boat down. He powered it toward the sandy beach. Down the shore, Amy could see a white cotton tent stretched over a rough, wooden frame. The camp belonged to her Aunt Edna and Uncle Joe. Drying racks full of dried fish were outside. Aunt Edna was waving at them with a dirty dish towel. She had a scarf on her head to keep mosquitoes away, and was wearing a summer parka soiled with fish blood and who knows what else.

Amy loved her aunt, as she was round and funny and reminded her of her mom. She laughed a lot and liked to tell jokes. They would set up camp together and fish for the rest of the week as a family.

Amy's dad, George, came out and waved at them. He helped Uncle Joe pull the boat up to shore. Amy got out and gave her dad a big hug. Isaac jumped up and down with joy and Sam was happy to see his dad. They all walked toward the tent and sat down to eat dinner.

Amy went to the willows behind the house and was able to change into some dry clothes. She was warmer, and hunger made her stomach growl. Hot fish soup, Pilot Bread crackers and coffee were on the table.

The fun of camping was going to start! Her cousins were there and they chatted happily while they ate the hot soup. They couldn't wait to explore camp.

After the late lunch, Amy tucked the purse and ulu in her coat and left it in the tent. She went out to play. It was the highlight of the summer to go to fish camp. It was fun because her cousins, two girls, a boy, and Amy, were good friends. They started playing tag, laughing and running through the camp and trees.

The next morning was warm and Amy and her mom cut up their catch of fish with ulus, to dry out on the racks in the sun. The fillets hung like laundry on the lines and Amy was happy to see all the food they would have for the winter. They would store it up for the long winter.

Amy thought about the skin bag with the ulu inside the tent.

"Mom, did you find out who lost the ulu…the one I found?"

"No, but I will ask around. Did you bring it here?" Mom asked.

"Yes, because I wanted to ask you about something on it. I wanted to find out about the words. I wasn't sure what they mean. I was really afraid that it belonged to someone who used it for bad power."

"What do you mean?" Amy's mom asked.

"The words on it say, 'Whoever holds this, holds power.'" Amy replied.

"Oh." Amy's mom said. "Bring it here."

Amy ran into the tent and pulled it out of the blankets where she had hidden it to show her mom.

Amy's mom read the words and said, "I will ask Uncle Abe. He'll know about it. He knows everyone in the village."

She was still looking it over when Amy's dad, George, came up to them.

"Come on, Amy. I want to show you something," he motioned.

She followed him down to the shore and they got into their boat again. They motored up the river to a small inlet. He slowed the boat down and they came to a narrow place where the willows were thick by the bank of the river. He stopped the boat and told her to look down and keep quiet. They waited awhile and then she saw them.

There was a muskrat family swimming near the boat. Their sleek brown fur was so smooth and shiny.

"Watch quietly," he whispered.

The female muskrat swam under the boat with two baby muskrats following her.

"There are two families of muskrats here. I saw a bigger one yesterday with her babies." Amy's dad said quietly.

The babies looked like little wet furry puppies. They were so cute! Amy wanted to reach out and touch them, but they swam by quickly and disappeared into the reeds near the shore.

Dad chuckled and said, "We will leave them alone. They will grow up and there will be many more muskrats for later."

They watched for awhile and then Dad put a fishing line over the side of the boat. Grayling fish were swarming around the boat and he pulled in six large fish for dinner in just a few minutes.

When they got back, Amy and her mom swiftly took the ulus and sliced the fish. The ulus were so sharp that they could cut between the skin and meat of the grayling. They sliced it up quickly and put the pieces of fish into a pot to boil for soup.

Sharp ulus could cut anything. Amy and her mom used their ulus everyday. Her mom had taught Amy to slice meat and fish up and have it ready to cook in no time! Amy used one of her mom's ulus, but she had always wanted her own.

She thought about keeping the one she found, but she knew that she needed to find out whose it was and give it back to the owner. That is what her mom taught her-to be honest.

The fish pieces boiling in the pot smelled delicious. They added onions, garlic, rice, salt and pepper and it was steaming. Amy felt her stomach rumble with hunger. She was starving!

Abe hobbled over to the pot and put some wood on the fire. Amy wanted to ask him about the ulu. She ran to get it.

"Uncle Abe, I found this yesterday by the lagoon. It was there in the willows, by the water. Do you know whose it is? "

Abe wrinkled his nose, pushed back his glasses and examined the ulu. He looked at for a long time and turned it over in his hands. He didn't say a thing. He seemed to be studying the words for awhile. Amy impatiently hopped on one foot and the other, waiting for his answer.

Finally, Abe sat down, ulu in his hand and said to Amy, "Sit down here. I know whose it is and I will tell you a story about it."

Amy was surprised and listened as Abe began his story.

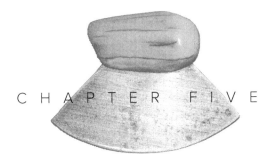

Ulu Tales

A be began his story:

"A long time ago, there was a young man from the village of Buckland who wanted to get married. He loved a young woman from this village. Her father was an elder there, was a good hunter, and was very respected.

The young man was from a very poor family. He didn't have anything to offer the girl or her family, except he did have a kind heart and he was a good son to his mother. He always took good care of his mother and helped his brothers and sisters. He thought about how to win the love of the young woman he loved and he came up with an idea.

He decided he would go hunting and bring back muskrat and fox furs and ask his mother to make a warm, beautiful parka to give as a gift for the young woman. He thought about how happy she would be, and he wanted to make her feel special. He wanted to impress her and her father and mother, and to show how well he would take care of her, if she married him.

After he left to hunt, another young man from the village heard of this plan and decided that he also wanted to marry this same girl, but he was known to have a hard and evil heart. He was selfish and often drank too much alcohol and he hurt others with his actions and words.

He made a plan to pretend and act as if he had changed, at least until the young woman believed him. He even fooled himself, telling himself that he was a great man. He blamed his parents for the problems and troubles he had.

So he approached the young woman. He brought her good things to eat everyday, offered to take her on his sled to places she wanted to go and told her that she was very beautiful. He brought fresh meat to her father and mother and tried to show them how much better he was than the other young man who desired her.

The young woman remembered his reputation, *but he seemed to be* very nice to her. After awhile, she finally started to think that he was a good man and had changed from his past mistakes. Her parents and some people of the village told her that he was fooling her and that she should stay away from him, but she didn't listen to their advice.

She thought to herself, *since he is nice to me, he must have changed. I am sure he is better now…people just don't understand him like I do.*

Now the other young man finally returned with the furs and his mother went to work to sew a beautiful parka with mittens to match. It would be a wonderful gift for the young woman. The mother worked many long hours on it and finally, it was done!

The young man was so pleased and excited to show the young woman the gifts. He smiled as he walked to her house with the parka and mittens. He greeted her and gave them to her. He had so much happiness in his heart that he was smiling. He presented the gifts to the young woman. She was surprised by his generosity and very happy with the parka and mittens and thanked him.

He told her that he and his family wanted to welcome her into his family and he asked her if she would marry him.

'You are the most beautiful woman in the village!' the young man said. 'I will love you with all of my heart.'

He promised her that he would do his best to make her happy. He admitted that he was poor but that he would work hard to make a good life for them.

She didn't answer him with either a 'yes' or 'no' because she was confused about who to marry.

After he left, she told her mother and father about the proposal. She said she couldn't decide which man she should marry as both of them seemed genuine. Her feelings were unsure and confused.

Her mother heard the whole story and then told her to wait and she would give her a gift which would help her decide. While she went to get the gift, her father asked her to think about the man she would choose carefully, as it would affect her life.

Her mother went to her sewing bag, and got out a bone needle, sinew thread, thimble and an ulu. On the ulu, she inscribed these words:

'For the Word of God is is quick and powerful.

He who holds this, holds power. Hebrews 4:12.'

Her mother said for her to think about these words.

She said, 'These words will help you with this decision. It will also show you about other decisions in your life.'

She paused to let her think about it.

Then she said, 'The needle, thread and thimble will remind you that choices in life are like pieces of skin that you sew together to make mukluks or mittens. If you use weak furs, you will have a parka that will tear. If you use strong furs, you will have strong, good parka.'

The mother picked up her old Bible and read:

'For the word of God is alive and powerful. It is sharper than the sharpest two-edged sword, cutting between soul and spirit, between joint and marrow. It exposes our innermost thoughts and desires.' (Hebrews 4:12)

The girl knew that a sword was something like an ulu, a long knife that is sharp like an ulu. She had often used her mom's ulu to cut through joint, marrow and the skin on caribou meat. It sliced sharply and cleanly, separating the waste from the good meat, so that she could throw away the bad stuff and keep the good parts to eat.

After that, the girl thought about that saying it for many days. She finally knew what to do and was able to decide who she should marry."

Abe paused to let Amy think about it. "She always kept the ulu as a reminder," Abe finished.

Abe smiled and Amy looked at him with surprise and asked, "But, what does the story mean? I don't understand! What did she decide? How did the verse help her decide?"

Amy wasn't sure what to think.

C H A P T E R   S I X

Discovery of Real Power

"**U**NCLE!**"** Amy squealed with excitement, "how did the ulu help her? Which man did she marry?"

"So many questions!" Abe answered. "I will tell you about the verse, and how it helped her, and then maybe you will understand more of the story."

Abe smiled before continuing, "She chose the young man who had a kind heart, with confidence. Because of her choice, she lived with much love and kindness and he did make her very happy.

They didn't have much at first, but later, they found many blessings coming their way. They had eight children and many grandchildren. When she was old, the young man loved her just like he did when she was young and beautiful. He became a respected elder in the village and she became an elder too."

"What happened to the other man?" Amy asked.

Abe replied, "He became angry when young woman refused to marry him. He soon got married to another woman, but not for love. He treated his wife very badly and she was sad and lonely until she died. He also died without giving or having true love and was lost on a hunting trip in the winter."

Abe said, "You asked, how did the words on the ulu help the woman? I will tell you. The words reminded her to get wisdom for her decisions from God."

Abe let that sink in before continuing,

"God's Word works in our hearts like an ulu. She separated what she thought was good from what was not truly good."

Abe was quiet for a moment, then went on,

"The way she did that was to remember the Word of God when making a decision."

"She would make her choices, only after she prayed and read God's Word, and asked God for His wisdom. She would listen to His voice and follow what she believed she heard," Abe explained.

"She was then able to cut between good and bad decisions, just like cutting with your ulu between bone and marrow. Bone is not good to eat, but marrow is!" Able chuckled at his little joke.

He continued again,

"The young woman *sewed together her choices* and made a good life from those decisions, just like making a good parka out of good furs. She kept a bone needle, sinew and thimble to remind her of that lesson."

Amy was quiet for a minute, thinking about all of that. It was a lot to think about.

"So, why does the ulu I found say, "Whoever holds this, holds power?" She asked.

"Ahh…" Abe said.

"When you make choices, if you follow God's Word, you will have power in life."

Abe continued, "Your life will turn out according to your choices, good or bad. Like bad meat, a bad decision can make you sick."

"Now, I see it!" Amy said.

She looked at the Abe with respect.

"So, whose ulu is this?" Amy asked with awe.

Abe smiled. "I know whose it is," he answered.

"And she does have real power."

CHAPTER SEVEN

Decisions for Amy

T he next day, Amy rode in their boat with her dad, brother and cousin further up the river to fish. They had set nets* along the bank in the river. They stopped by the first one to bring in the catch of fish. The net was full with shimmering, squiggly, fish. They hauled it on the boat, picked out the fish and threw the net back into the water.

Amy loved doing this and the sun warmed her flannel shirt as she worked. Her dad was all business and they worked hard for several hours without a break.

Amy swatted mosquitoes all morning. The sun seemed to bring them out in swarms. She already had bites on her legs, even though she was wearing jeans. They felt like they were biting her through her clothes. Mosquitoes were a part of summer camp, but she didn't like them.

When they got back, Amy's mom was cooking caribou stew. Amy helped her dad clean the fish and hang them on the rack to dry. When they were done, Amy went to play with her cousins. They played *Hide and Seek* and *Kick the Can*. After about an hour, they walked back to the camp to eat the yummy caribou stew and warm sourdough homemade bread that her mom had made. It was delicious and made her feel satisfied and happy.

Amy grew sleepy after her busy day. She went into the tent to go to sleep. The camp grew quiet and everyone slipped into their sleeping bags. The night was still and cool. Amy heard a lonely owl hooting as she drifted off to sleep. It was still light outside and Aukluk, her puppy, curled up by her side and starting snoring.

The next day dawned bright and warm. Amy stretched out in her sleeping bag and realized it was Sunday. Her mom and dad didn't fish on Sunday since they usually went to church and relaxed with their family. Amy loved Sundays. Amy's dad would read to them from their Bible and then the rest of the day was for rest and relaxation.

Everyone was taking it easy and Amy's mom got up and made some sourdough pancakes and cocoa. They rolled the sour pancake with butter and sugar inside, which made it a treat. The hot cocoa, loaded with sugar, made Amy feel energized and ready to play with her cousins.

After breakfast, Amy and the cousins decided to take a walk up the creek from their camp. They were hoping to see some beavers or muskrats and pick flowers. They walked along, keeping an eye out for wildlife. Aukluk ran ahead, set free from his leash and collar. He was excited and ran ahead too far. Amy called him, but he kept running. He was a young dog and wasn't trained well yet. He was always disappearing!

Amy loved him and knew that one day when he was trained, he might lead a dog team. For now, Amy just had to keep him out of trouble and teach him who was the boss by making him obey her.

Amy heard Aukluk suddenly bark wildly. She ran, looking for him and when she rounded the corner, to her dismay, Aukluk was crouched oddly on the ground. As she ran closer, she could see that he was whining and pawing at his nose. His nose had quills protruding out of it! He was crying and rolling on the ground to try to get them out. Amy quickly looked around for the obvious porcupine that had tangled with Aukluk, but it was already gone.

"Oh, Aukluk," she sighed, "You really got in trouble this time!"

She tried to pull on one of the quills, but Aukluk yelped louder, so she stopped and looked around for help. Aukluk rolled wildly on the ground, trying to dislodge the porcupine quills.

Her cousin turned to her, "We have to go and get your dad!"

Amy looked at her. She couldn't leave Aukluk alone out there and she wasn't sure how to get him back to camp.

"You go," Amy ordered. "I can stay here until you get back."

"No!" Amy's cousin said. "It is too dangerous. There are bears out here."

Amy thought about that. She was not sure if she really wanted to stay alone, after all.

"How about if we carry Aukluk back?" She asked.

"We can try." Amy's cousin agreed.

Both girls tried to pick up the squirming dog. Aukluk snapped at them, wiggled and jumped out of their arms. He was a mess of quills and there were some hanging off of his legs. He was snarling, biting at his quills and whining. This wasn't going to work!

Amy wrinkled her nose, and tried to think about what to do. She decided to call Aukluk to follow them back, but he was too distracted to walk with his pain.

Amy stood there thinking. She remembered Abe's story about the ulu. She wasn't sure how to do it, but she quickly prayed,

"Jesus, if you can help me get Aukluk back to camp, show me how. Help me to figure this out!"

She had to make a decision here, whether to leave Aukluk alone and take a chance that he would get lost or stay there beside him and be alone in the wilderness with bears and wolves and who knows what there was out there.

She quietly prayed and asked God to show her the best decision so that she could throw away the bad one.

She was quiet for a few minutes, thinking. She tried to listen to her thoughts. The mosquitoes hummed and Aukluk whined and cried as she waited. She was trying hard to hear God speak. She had never tried it before. She decided to stay quiet until she got an answer. Her thoughts whirled.

Amy's cousin looked at Aukluk with pity.

"Poor puppy. Poor puppy," she softly comforted him.

Suddenly, Amy knew what to do. A clear thought had come to her mind. She told her cousin her plan.

She whipped off her scarf and tied it around Aukluk's two front legs, while her cousin used her scarf to tie the pup's two back legs together. Now, he really was an unhappy puppy! Aukluk whined and howled with sadness and tried to jerk free. Amy took off her jacket and laid it on the ground. They picked Aukluk up and quickly laid him on the jacket like a medical patient. She lifted up both sides of the jacket like a stretcher and her cousin took the other side, and they and headed for camp with Aukluk on top. Aukluk tried to squirm off, but Amy held his collar tight with her hand. After a few minutes, he settled down and just whined while they walked back to camp.

Later, at the tent, Amy's dad removed the quills one by one, while Amy fed Aukluk pieces of meat to comfort him after each painful pull on the quills with the pliers. Finally, her dad got them all out.

Amy's dad told the girls they did the right thing, and Aukluk would be fine. Sure enough, afterwards, Aukluk jumped up with delight, happy to be done with the ordeal and seemed quite humbled by the experience. He hung close to the tent and stayed by Amy's feet for the rest of that evening.

That night, Amy crawled into bed, and felt the ulu in the bag under her blanket. She smiled. God had used His ulu to show her the way. This made her wonder about the owner of the ulu again. She had to ask Abe to take her to meet the owner!

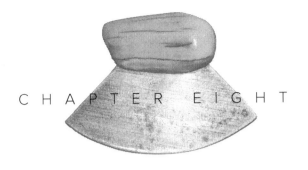

CHAPTER EIGHT

May and the Sewing Contest

Amy woke up the next morning, determined to ask Abe to take her to the person who owned the ulu.

Aukuk ran around in circles, jumping and barking with excitement. He even chased his tail. He seemed to have forgotten his misadventure from the previous day. He did stay close to camp, though.

Amy waited until Abe had finished his breakfast and coffee. Then she asked with excitement, "Uncle Abe, remember the ulu I found? Do you know where we should return it?"

Abe's face wrinkled up with a grin. He coughed, smiled, waited and finally made a grunt.

He really knew how to drag out an answer, she moaned inwardly.

"Tomorrow when we go to Kotzebue, I will take you to her." Abe said.

He turned back to his breakfast of fried bread, covered in sugar. He was dipping it in his black coffee.

Amy was impatient. "But, Uncle, can't you just tell me?" she whined.

He waited and said, "She will tell you herself… about the ulu."

Amy wanted to know! She also knew she would have to wait.

Dad saw her, and called her to get the fish net for the day and put it in the boat.

The next morning, Amy, Mom, Uncle Abe, her brothers and their two dogs piled into the boat for the trip back to Kotzebue. Dad was staying back at camp to keep fishing with Aunt Edna and Uncle Joe for another week. Uncle Abe drove the boat.

The crossing of Kobuk Lake was easier this time. The day was bright and chilly, but the wind had quieted down. That made the trip less wet and choppy. They got back to Kotzebue in late afternoon, unloaded the boat and headed for home. Mom quickly made some fried meat, and added dried fish and some muktuk from the spring catch. They had canned fruit cocktail for dessert.

Amy felt cozy and warm and happy to stretch out in her own bed that night. She slept like a polar bear in the winter, warm and cozy, in a deep sleep. She dreamed about the ulu. It was in the hand of a woman. She was cutting meat, but then the ulu turned into a book with gold writing and it was shining.

The next day, Abe called Amy and announced,

"I am going to see my friend. Bring the ulu."

Amy jumped out of bed, and quickly got dressed. She gulped down some bread and butter, when she saw that Abe was ready to go and waiting for her by the door. They started walking across town, toward the lagoon.

Abe didn't say much and Amy wondered where they were going. They walked to the end of the road, and stopped by a small, weathered house. A snowmobile and sled sat outside the door. A fishing net hung over the sled, and some buckets of seal oil sat near the storm door. The strong smell of fish and seal oil mixed together hit their noses as they walked up.

At the door, Abe called out loudly, "May?"

A small, old woman opened the door and her wrinkled, brown face smiled with a toothless smile.

She sang out, "Addii!" * and chuckled with happiness to see Abe.

May opened the door and invited them in. She was shorter than Amy and looked very old. She was bent a little, but seemed strong also. Her grey hair was pulled back into two braids and wrapped up on her head. She wore a summer parka and faded shoes.

A small mutt with curly brown hair wiggled with delight by her feet and barked with excitement. She waved her hand at the dog, "Charley, go away." Charley barked again and ran in little circles, ignoring her.

May made some coffee and Amy sat down on the old wooden bed. Abe sat on the one red painted wood chair near the Formica table in the kitchen. A seal skin was stretched out in a large frame against the wall, in the process of being tanned.

May laid warm sourdough bread on the table. She brought out bowls of salmon berries* as a treat for dessert.

Abe talked to her about fishing, the weather, the fire and the fishing camp while Amy was impatient, waiting for the moment he would ask her about the ulu. He seemed to be chatting with May about everything else, but not the ulu.

Amy held the purse in her lap, hoping May would see it and recognize it. May just kept pouring more coffee, eating and talking with Abe.

Finally, Abe said,

"May, Amy found this by the lagoon."

He looked at Amy and raised his eyebrows to signal her. She held the ulu up, and May squinted over her glasses, peering at the purse.

"Addii," she grunted and looked away. Then she leaned over, petted Charlie, who was begging for a piece of dried fish.

"When you find it?" she finally asked quietly.

Amy replied, "On the Fourth of July. It was caught in a willow by the lagoon."

Abe continued "Amy wants to know about it."

May shifted.

"Ok," she answered.

She waited for a few moments and then said in broken English mixed with Inupiaq, "It was my mother's…from her mother. Her favorite ulu. She got it and pass it to me. It is good ulu."

Amy quickly handed the bag to May, who took it in her hands and opened the bag to pull out the ulu. She stroked the ulu softly, like a long lost pet. She smiled and asked Amy,

"You know words?"

Amy nodded. She was happy to hear more though.

"Abe told me the story," Amy answered. "Was that your mom who married the good man?"

"Yes, and she live good life," May said softly, trying to say it in her limited English. "She love God. She had powerful faith. She teach me. I live like that."

She chuckled with joy.

"Maybe I eat too much marrow and I get too fat." She said with amusement.

She laughed again at her own joke, because she was not fat at all. Her toothless grin made it seem even more hilarious.

She pulled the thimble, sinew and needle out of the purse.

"Still sharp." she muttered.

She tried on the thimble, and held the ulu to the window to read the words again. The words had some wear, but were still readable. She took her index finger and touched the words as if stroking them. It was clear that the ulu meant a lot to her. She sat looking at it for a few moments in silence. No one said anything.

"Ulu not lost." She remarked.

"It here when I cut fish," she continued.

"Maybe God want you find it. Maybe He have plan."

She seemed thoughtful. After a moment, she looked up and asked,

"Amy, you can sew?"

Amy nodded.

"You can make mittens from skin?"

Amy nodded again.

May continued,

"I want you make mittens for contest. You use bone needle and sinew. I give you good furs."

Amy's eyes grew big. "Really?"

"I help you," May said.

"One week and maybe we win prize."

Amy nodded with excitement. She loved the challenge. She couldn't wait to get started!

CHAPTER NINE

Mittens and Kittens

All week long, Amy and May worked the skin for the mittens. May was slow to choose only the best fur and the skins that were tanned soft enough for the project. Amy watched her as she worked the skin with the metal and wood tools to make it softer. In the end, the furs were cut and the pieces were laid out on cardboard to see how they would fit together.

May gave Amy pieces to sew together carefully using the bone needle and sinew. Amy separated strands of sinew that were tangled in a mass, threaded the needle and sewed the pieces together carefully as May had taught her. Amy's mom had taught her to sew well, but she was also learning from May's example.

May taught her in the old way. She told her to make the stitches close together so they didn't show. The design was beautiful. The small skin pieces sewn together contrasted in color and May showed Amy what small strips went with what pieces. Dark and light skins were sewn together with sinew to make the cuff, which was attached to the muskrat skin around the top. The thumbs and palm of the mittens had leather sewn into place.

Amy kept sewing and only stopped to eat and have some tea. At night, she went home and slept soundly. Each day when she came, they sewed, laughed at May's jokes and talked about the old ways.

She found out that May had grown up in Buckland, where her parents had moved, and she had married a young sled maker. They had three children. One lived in Anchorage, one lived in Kotzebue and one lived in Buckland with their families.

She told Amy many lively stories about her childhood, and stories of her life as a young woman. She told her of her adventures. She told her about her husband who had long since gone to Heaven and who had been a pastor and sled maker. He knew the old way of shaping the hardwood to his design with steam to make beautiful sled runners and curved handles. He always had the fastest sleds in the village and the most desired sleds to be bought.

She told Amy about picking blueberries on the tundra, herding reindeer with her husband and hunting for walruses on the sea. She told her about a time when they had been lost in a blizzard so strong that even the sled dogs were so afraid that they hid down in the snow to escape the wind. She told about how she had prayed with her husband and God had stopped the wind and cleared the air so they could see their way to go home. They made it safely to their cabin before the snow and whiteout * conditions came again, which then lasted for days.

Slowly the mittens were made. Amy cut the lining which was a soft white rabbit fur with a red calico trim and backing, and she sewed it inside out to make the rabbit fur line the mittens. Carefully sewing the two layers together, she was able to see each mitten come together to perfection.

With May's thoughtful eye and instruction, Amy beaded tiny red, blue and gold beads around the design on the cuff. The beads made star shapes and gave the mittens a delightful design.

The final work to finish the mittens was to take red yarn and braid the strands together to make a rope. They attached the red braid to the corners of each of the mittens to keep them together and to hang them after use.

It was late at night when they finished. They had worked on them for almost a week.

Amy stretched and stood up. "I'm so tired!" she sighed.

May smiled and said, "Then we will have tea!"

May pulled out some Pilot crackers and butter and poured some tea. They laid the mittens on the table and looked at them. May smiled with her toothless grin. They both knew they had a winner.

Amy stood up to give May a hug, but just then, Charlie started barking furiously. He ran to the window, growling and leaping at the window. Amy went over to see out and to her surprise, an orange cat looked back at her!

May and Amy looked at each other, surprised. Cats were not common, with all the dogs in town. The cat meowed, and walked along the window ledge outside. Amy opened the front door and went out. The cat was rubbing against the window and meowing sadly. She looked hungry. Amy tried to pick her up, but she jumped down and ran under the house. Amy squatted to see where she ran and to her amazement, three little orange and grey kittens were staring back at her!

"May! There are kittens!" Amy shouted.

May laughed.

"Addii!" she exclaimed again with surprise.

Amy reached under the house and pulled out a little wide-eyed orange-striped ball of fluff. He meowed in response. She pulled out the second one. He was white with grey stripes on his tail and back. As Amy reached for the last one, she saw that this one was orange-striped also, but he had long hair and white paws and was bigger than the other two. The mother meowed, watching Amy pick up her kittens.

"Okay, little mommy. I will bring you inside." Amy said to the mother cat.

She tucked the kittens inside her shirt, and brought them into the house, while the mother cat ran ahead to make sure her kittens were safe. She scooted inside and under the bed before Charlie could chase her. Amy looked at the helpless little bundles. She was excited about the kittens, but what would her mom think?

CHAPTER TEN

The Prize!

Amy gathered up the kittens and the mother cat and put them in a box to carry home. The largest kitten was a rascal and kept escaping, so she tucked him into the pocket of her parka. He snuggled deep down into it while she walked home. She carried the box carefully, holding the mother cat inside with the kittens. A bag with the new mittens was slung over her shoulder.

Amy burst in the door shouting, "Look Mom! I found these kittens under May's house. Aren't they cute?"

Mom was still up and jumped up from her chair. Amy brought the box to show her mom the kittens.

"Well, what are we going to do with these!" laughed Mom.

She petted the kittens and mother cat, who seemed anxious to get out of the box.

Amy settled the kittens in the box by the stove.

Mom said, "We'll talk about what to do with the kittens in the morning. Go to bed now, it's late!"

Amy was sleepy and wanted to climb into bed anyway.

The next morning, little meows came from the box, and all three kittens were there, wanting up and out of the box. The mother cat had figured out that she could climb in and out and that the kittens were safe in the box. She rubbed up against Amy's leg to say '*thank you*.'

Aukluk was amused and didn't seem to want to hurt the kittens, but he kept nosing them with doggy curiosity. The mother cat hissed at him and raced under the bed whenever he came near. Amy found some dried fish and tore off some for them, and both the mother and kittens devoured it.

Amy's mom left for work and her brothers were still asleep, so Amy had time to herself. She made some tea and oatmeal and sat down to admire the mittens that she and May had made. They were beautiful, warm and well done. She hoped she would win, but there were many women in the village who knew how to bead and sew well, so the competition would be tough.

Isaac woke up and was so excited to see the kittens. Amy showed him how to hold them, and they crawled around on his lap, much to his delight. He giggled constantly whenever they moved. She showed him how to hold and pet them softly.

Sam was still sleeping in, so he would have to see them later. He was missing out!

Right after lunch, Amy took Isaac and picked up the bag with the mittens and they headed to church to enter the mittens in the contest. There would be a potluck meal later and the judges would decide. She was nervous and excited. She knew there was a prize, but May hadn't told her what it was.

The church smelled good, with caribou stew and onions cooking together. Women were stirring big pots, and some of the men were cutting up some fresh fish and dropping it into pots to cook and the windows of the church were steaming up. It all seemed warm and like home to Amy. She saw that Abe had joined the men, and was taking some fresh muktuk out to cut up.

There were kids running around and some tables were set up with the sewing that was to be judged. Amy walked around looking at each entry. There were mukluks, jade jewelry, fur slippers, mittens, parka covers, and some art with baleen. * The sewing contest was for items that had been made by hand.

Amy took Isaac outside to play and she joined a group of girls who were waiting for their moms inside. Amy was waiting for her mom too, because she was going to get off early from work and join them. After a few minutes, she saw May walking slowly up to the church. May smiled her toothless smile and waved. May joined the other women in the church to help with the cooking.

Mom came with Sam. He ran off to join his friends, and Amy took mom in to show her all the things that were to be shown to the judge.

"Do you think I have a chance?" Amy asked.

"Of course!" Mom answered.

At four pm, the judges started walking around and taking notes in their little writing pads. They looked carefully at everything and took a long time. Amy anxiously waited for the announcement. It would be announced at dinner.

Meanwhile Amy ran home to check on the kittens. They were nursing and looked very happy. She was hoping to keep them, or at least one of them!

Dinner had started by the time she got back. Everyone was talking and eating, and it was steaming in the church. Soup was served, both salmon soup and caribou stew, dried fish, muktuk and some berries. There was fried chicken and some green beans, a real treat. Eskimo ice-cream* came out and that was loved by everyone!

After awhile, Uncle Abe got up slowly and walked to the front.

"I want to announce the winners," he said. He paused, coughed, and took a long time. Amy remembered how he like to wait until everyone was impatient to make his story more exciting.

He listed off the winners for each category. Right when he got to the sewing contest, he paused and winked at Amy. She squirmed.

Did that mean she won or was he teasing her? she wondered.

"Today, we have a winner for the sewing contest," he said. "But, we have a tie…Our winner is…" He paused again.

"Jewel Jones, for her slippers, and Amy Peters, for her mittens!" he announced.

Amy screamed with delight and jumped up. She ran over to hug May who was smiling.

Abe called both winners up, and gave them an envelope. Inside, Amy saw $250! She squealed with happiness. She couldn't believe it. She ran over to Mom, who was smiling too. What a surprise!

She sat down, so happy. She had already decided to give May part of the money for helping her. She pulled out $50 to give May, but something didn't feel right. Her heart was tingling. She could see May's little humble house in her mind. It was one of those clear thoughts. *Maybe it was God speaking again,* she thought. She felt uneasy. She pulled out another $50, and felt a little better, but not completely at peace.

What should she do? Her mind raced. All she could hear was May's voice in her mind, telling her stories about her children and husband and the old ways. She really didn't know what to do. She didn't know what to think! She said a little prayer and waited and thought about what God was saying.

Right away, she felt a strong thought of what to do.

She walked over to May and took her hands and said,

"May, this is all for you. I want you to have it, all of it."

May looked up and smiled. She took Amy's hands and clasped them.

"Oh! Praise God!" she said with a sweet look and her eyes twinkled with joy.

"I wouldn't have known how to do it, without you." Amy continued, with sincerity.

Just when Amy turned to walk back, May grabbed her shirt to stop her. Amy turned around to her.

"Here, Amy. I brought prize for you." May said, smiling.

Amy looked and to her astonishment, May was holding out the sealskin bag with her special ulu, needle, thread and thimble inside. May chuckled with delight.

"You already have prize you earn." May said.

Amy was wide-eyed.

This was May's most prized possession! she thought with surprise. *She is giving me her ulu!*

May said, "I give you. You learn already. You keep. It give you much joy. You keep for your family."

May smiled broadly as she handed it to Amy.

Amy reached down to take the bag with great love and hugged May softly with tears in her eyes.

This was the real prize-May, her new friend, who had taught her so much and the joy she felt, she thought.

The ulu was a prize, yes, but the love she felt for May, this deep love, was the biggest prize she could have imagined! She got it from following the words inscribed on the ulu given to her.

She saw her mom and waved at her. Mom came over, and told Amy,

"I am so proud of you."

"Does this mean I can keep the kittens?" Amy asked with a smile.

Amy's mom laughed and said,

"We'll see about that. Maybe May wants a kitten!"

May laughed. "Ah nee!" she said. "Charlie no like, but I like all right."

"Ok, May, I will share," Amy said. "I will bring you a kitten."

Amy looked around at her family, Abe and May. She felt warm love fill her heart. The contest didn't matter anymore.

What really mattered was love.

Continuing following Amy's adventures
as she finds herself marooned on an island!

Amy's Basket

By Linda L. Beck